Preface

The person [...]
of the cities [...]

Duke of Wellington the Marq[ue]ss
of Douro & Lord Wellesle
the city is the Glass town
Henry O'Donell ~~[illegible]~~
and Alexander Delancy are
Captain Tarry not at home
& Monsieur Like to live in
lonely places

Charlotte Brontë

August the 1st
1829

The Search
After
Hapiness

The Search After Hapiness

A TALE BY
Charlotte Brontë

Illustrated by
Carolyn Dinan

Simon & Schuster

Introduction

In December 1830, Branwell Brontë, then thirteen years old, began to set down in a work grandiloquently entitled "The History of The Young Men from Their First Settlement to The Present Time" a meticulously detailed account of the game of make-believe which had occupied himself and his three sisters for the past four years. From this, and from an account written by Charlotte entitled "The Twelve Adventurers", we learn that in June 1826 their father brought back from Leeds a box of twelve wooden soldiers, which he left beside Branwell's bed. In the morning the four children each excitedly chose one soldier for their own, Charlotte naming hers the "Duke of Wellington", Emily's being called "Gravey", and Anne's "Waiting Boy", while Branwell selected "Buonaparte". The children, imaginative and brilliant, but isolated in a remote moorland parsonage with no other companions of their own age, played almost to the exclusion of other interests at devising an imaginary land which their twelve heroes, or the "Young Men", as they called them, might conquer and colonize, and where they might rule over an ever larger and more diversified society. The location and topography of the new land were inspired by the African section of the Reverend J. Goldsmith's *A Grammar of General Geography* 1823. The wooden soldiers

[5]

sailed to "Ashantee" where, having conquered the natives, they built a city situated "in the middle of a large plain, bounded on the north by high mountains, on the south by the sea, on the east by gloomy forests, and on the west by evil deserts. . . . To the north the Gibble Kumri or Mountains of the Moon seemed a misty girdle to the plain of Dahomey; to the south the ocean guarded the coasts of Africa . . . to the west lay the desert". The city was called "Glass Town", a name apparently suggested by the glassy smooth water in an illustration of a port found in a book of travel. Inspired by the "Arabian Nights", the children constituted themselves the four Genii who presided over the fortunes of the inhabitants of the Glass Town Confederacy, or Verdopolitans as they were also called (Branwell's father was instructing him in Greek and Latin). While Branwell amused himself by describing minutely the history and geography of Glass Town, Charlotte threw herself into the production of literary works and magazines, most of them ascribed to various Verdopolitans.

"The Search after Hapiness", composed when Charlotte was thirteen, and written out in a minute hand in imitation of print, is not strictly part of the history of Glass Town. Charlotte's Preface, however, states that the action is set in Glass Town, and her heroes the Duke of Wellington and his sons play an important part. The Genii appear, and Dahomey is mentioned. The style and plot of the story are naturally influenced by Charlotte's reading. The children seem to have had no books intended for their own age, but to have devoured their father's library. When she wrote "The Search after Hapiness" Charlotte had read, among many other things, Milton's *Paradise Lost*, Byron's *Childe Harold* and, of course, the *Arabian Nights*.

"The Search after Hapiness" is, in its own right, a charming and quaint tale written by a talented child. It, and the many others like it, however, have another interest. They help to explain what would otherwise appear a miracle, that the three daughters of a humble clergyman who had hardly ever left a remote village should come to publish novels two of which are among the greatest in the language. As Miss Fannie Ratchford pointed out in *The Brontë's Web of Childhood* 1941, characters and situations from the childhood games were even used in the novels of Charlotte's maturity. "The Search after Hapiness" and its fellows are the evidence of the long and painstaking apprenticeship served by the future novelists.

In this edition Charlotte's own spelling and punctuation have been retained, except where this would affect the sense, or where it is the result of a slip of the pen.

The original manuscript has no illustrations and the water-colours for this edition have been provided by a young artist: Carolyn Dinan. Her work captures the mood of the story in a way that Charlotte Brontë would surely have approved.

T.A.J. BURNETT

Preface

The persons meant by the Chief of the city and his Sons
are the Duke of Wellington the Marquis of Duro and
Lord Wellesly. The city is the Glass town. Henry O'Donell
and Alexander Delancy are Captain Tarry-not-at-home
and Monsieur Like-to-live-in-lonely-places.

Charlotte Bronte
August the 17 1829

Contents

Chapter   I   Character of O Donell. Cause of his
travels.   13

the II   Set out. Meeting Delancy. Coming to
the old castle. Entering the new
world. Description.   18

the III   Coming to the cave. Maner of life.
Arrival of the old man.   27

the IV   Old man's tale.   32

the V   Departure of the old man.
Disapearance of Delancy.
Transportation of O Donell.
His arrival at the city.
His arrival at the palace.
His interview with his cheif.
He finds Delancy. End.   40

The Search After Hapiness

A Tale by
C B July 28 1829

Chapter I

Not many years ago there lived in a certain city a person
of the name of Henry O Donell, in figure he was tall of a
dark complexion and searching black eye, his mind was
strong and unbending his disposition unsociable and
though respected by many he was loved by few. The city
where he resided was very great and magnificent. It was
governed by a warior a mighty man of valour whose
deeds had resounded to the ends of the earth. This
soldier had two sons who were at that time of the
seperate ages of six and seven years. Henry O Donell was
a nobleman of great consequence in the city and a peculiar
favourite with the governor before whose glance his
stern mind would bow and at his comand O Donell's
selfwill would be overcome and while playing with the
young Princes he would forget his usual sulleness of
demeanour. The days of his childhood returned upon

him and he would be as merry as the youngest who was gay indeed. One day at court a quarrel ensued between him and another noble. Words came to blows and O Donell struck his oponent a violent blow on the left cheek. At this the miliatry King started up and commanded O Donell to apologize. This he imediatly did, but from that hour the spell of discontent seemed to have been cast over him and he resolved to quit the city. The evening before he put this resolution into practise he had an interview with the King and returned quite an altered man. Before he seemed stern and intractable now he was only meditative and sorrowful. As he was passing the inner court of the palace he perceived the two young princes at play. He called them and they came runing to him. "I am going far from this city and shall most likely never see you again" said O Donell. "Where are you going?" "I canot tell". "Then why do you go away from us why do you go from your own house and lands from this great and splendid city to you know not where?"

"Because I am not happy here". "And if you are not happy here where you have every thing for which you can whish do you expect to be happy when you are dying of hunger or thirst in a desert or longing for the society of men when you are thousands of miles from any human being?" "How do you know that that will be my case?" "It is very likely that it will". "And if it was I am determined to go". "Take this then that you may sometimes rember us when you dwell with only the wild beast of the desert or the great eagle of the mountain" said they as they each gave him a curling lock of their hair. "Yes I will take it my princes and I shall rember you and the mighty warrior King your father even when the angel of Death has stretched forth his bony arm against me and I am within the confines of his dreary Kingdom the cold damp grave" replied O Donell as the tears rushed to his eyes and he once more embraced the little princes and then quitted them it might be for ever. . . .

Chapter the II

The Dawn of the next morning found O Donell on the sumit of a High mountain which overlooked the city. He had stopped to take a farewell view of the place of his nativity. All along the eastern horizon there was a rich glowing light which as it rose gradually melted into the pale blue of the sky in which just over the light there was still visible the silver crescent of the moon. In a short time the sun began to rise in golden glory casting his splendid radiance over all the face of nature and illuminating the magnificent city in the midst of which towering in silent grandeur there appeared the Palace where dwelt the mighty Prince of that great and beautiful city all around the brazen gates and massive walls of which there flowed the majestic stream of the Guadima whose Banks were bordered by splendid palaces and magnificent gardens. Behind these stretching for many a league were fruitful plains and forests whose shade seemed almost impenetrable to a single ray of light while in the distance blue mountains were seen raising their heads to the sky and forming a misty girdle to the plains of Dahomey. On

the whole of this grand and beautiful prospect O Donell's gaze was long and fixed but his last look was to the palace of the King and a tear stood in his eye as he said ernestly "May he be preserved from all evil may good attend him and may the cheif Geni spread their broad sheild of protection over him all the time of his sojourn in this wearisome world. Then turning round he began to decend the mountain. He pursued his way till the sun began to wax hot when he stopped and sitting down he took out some provisions which he had brought with him and which consisted of a few biscuits and dates. While he was eating a tall man came up and acosted him. O Donell requested him to sit beside him and offered him a biscuit. This he refused and taking one out of a small bag which he carried he sat down and they began to talk. In the course of conversation O Donell learnt that this man's name was Alexander De Lancy that he was a native of France and that he was engaged in the same pursuit with himself i.e. the search of happiness. They talked for a long time and at last agreed to travel together. Then rising they pursued their journey. Towards night fall they lay down in the open air and slept soundly till morning when they again set off and thus they continued till the third day when about two hours after noon they aproached an old castle which they entred and as they were examining it they discovered a subteaneous passage which they could not see the end of. "Let us follow where this passage leads us and perhaps we may find happiness

here" said O Donell. Delancy agreed the two stepped into the opening imediatly a great stone was rolled to the mouth of the passage with a noise like thunder which shut out all but a single ray [of] daylight. "What is that?!" exclaimed O Donell. "I cannot tell", replied DeLancy "but never mind I suppose it is only some genius playing tricks." "Well it may be so" returned O Donell and they proceeded on their way. After traveling for a long time as near as they could reckon about two days they perceived a silvery streak of light on the walls of the passage something like the light of the moon. In a short time they came to the end of the passage and leaping out of the opening which formed it they entred a new world. They were at first so much bewildred by the different objects which struck their senses that they almost fainted but at length recovering they had time to see everything around them. They were upon the top of a rock which was more than a thousand fathoms high. All beneath them was liquid Mountains tossed to and fro with horrible confusion roaring and raging with a tremendous noise and crowned with waves of foam. All above them was a mighty firmament in one part covered with black clouds from which darted huge and terrible sheets of Lightning. In another part an imense globe of Light like silver was hanging in the sky and several smaller globes which spakled exceedingly surounded it. In a short time the tempest which was dreadful beyond description ceased the large black clouds

cleared away the silver globes vanished and another globe whose light was of a gold coulour appeared. It was far larger than the former and in a little time it became so intensely bright that they could no longer gaze on it. So after looking around them for some time they rose and pursued their journey. They had travelled a long way when they came [to] an imense forest the trees of which bore a large fruit of a deep purple colour of which they tasted and found that it was fit for food. They journeyed in this forest for three days and on the third day they entred a valley or rather a deep glen surounded on each side by tremendous rocks whose tops were lost in the clouds. In this glen they continued for some time and at last came in sight of a mountain which rose so high that they could not see the sumit though the sky was quite clear. At the foot of the mountain there flowed a river of pure water bordered by trees which had flowers of a beautiful rose coulour. Except these trees nothing was to be seen but black forests and huge rocks rising out of a wilderness which bore the terrible aspect of devastation and which stretched as far as the eye could reach. In this desolate land no sound was to be heard, not even [the] cry of the eagle or the scream of the Curlew but a silence like the silence of the grave reigned over all the face of nature unbroken except by the murmur of the river as it slowly wound its course through the desert.

Chapter the III

After they had contemplated this scene for some time O Donell exclaimed "ALEXANDER. Let us abide here. What need have we to travel farther? Let us make this our place of rest!". "We will" replied De Lancy "and this shall be our abode" added he pointing to a cave at the foot of the mountains. "It shall" returned O Donell as they entred it. In this country they remained for many long years and passed their time in a maner which made them completely happy. Sometimes they would sit upon a high rock and listen to the hoarse thunder rolling through the sky and making the mountains to echo and the deserts to ring with its awful voice, somtimes they would watch the lightning darting across black clouds and shivering huge fragments of rock in its terrible passage sometimes they would witness the great glorious orb of gold sink behind the far distant mountains which girded the horizon and then watch the advance of grey twilight and the little stars coming forth in beauty and the silver moon arising in her splendour till the cold dews of night began to fall and then they would retire to their bed in the cave with hearts full of joy and thankfulness. One evening they were seated in this cave by a large Blazing fire of turf which cast its lurid light to the high arched roof and illuminated the tall and stately pillars cut by the hand of nature out [of] the stony rock with a red and cheerful glare that appeared strange in this desolate land which no fires had ever before visited except those feirce flames of death which flash from the heavens when robed in the dreadful majesty of thunder. They were seated in this cave then listening to the howling night wind as it swept in mournful cadences through the trees of the forest which encircled the foot of the mountain and bordered the stream which flowed round it. They were quite silent and their thoughts were ocupied by those that were afar off and whom it was their fate most likely never more to behold. O Donell was thinking of his noble master and his young Princes of the thousands of miles which intervened between him and them and the sad silent tear gushed forth as he ruminated on the happiness of those times when his master frowned not when the gloom of care gave place to the smile of freindship when he would talk to him and laugh with him and be to him not as a brother no no but as a mighty warrior who relaxing from his haughtiness would now and then converse with his high officers in a strain of vivacity and playful humour not to be eaqualled. Next he viewed him in his mind's eye at the head of his army. He heard in the ears of his imagination

[28]

the buzz of expectation of hope and supposition which humed round him as his penetrating eye with a still keeness of expression was fixed on the distant ranks of the enemy. Then he heard his authorative voice exclaim "Onward brave sons of freedom onward to the battle" and lastly his parting words to him "In prosperity or in misery in sorrow or in joy in populous cities or in desolate wildernesses my prayer shall go with you" darted across his mind with such painful distinctness that he at length gave way to his uncontrollable greif at the thought that he should never behold his beloved and mighty comander more and burst into a flood of tears. "What is the matter Henry?" exclaimed Delancy. "O nothing nothing" was the reply and they were resuming their tacit thinking when a voice was heard outside the cavern which broke strangely upon the desolate silence of that land which for thousands of years had heard no sound save the howling of the wind through the forest the echoing of the thunder among mountains or the solitary murmuring of the river if we except the presence of O Donell and Delancy. "Listen!" cried ALEXANDER "listen! What is that?" "It is the sound of a man's voice" replied Henry and then snatching up a burning torch he rushed to the mouth of the cave followed by Delancy. When they had got there they saw the figure of a very old man sitting on the damp wet ground moaning and complaining bitterly. They went up to him. At their approach he rose and said "Are you human or supernatural beings?". They assured him that they were human. He went on "Then why have you taken up your abode in this land of the grave?" O Donell answered that he would relate to him all the particulars if he would take shelter for the night with them. The old man consented and when they were all assembled round the cheerful fire O Donell fulfilled his promise and then requested the old man to tell them how he came to be travelling there. He complied and began as follows. . . .

Chapter the IV

"I was the son of a respectable merchant in Moussoul. My father intended to bring me up to his own trade but I was idle and did not like it. One day as I was playing in the street a very old man came up to me and asked me if I would go with him. I asked him where he was going. He replyed that if I would go with him he would show me very wonderful things. This raised my curiosity and I consented. He imediatly took me by the hand and hurried me out of the city of Moussoul so quickly that my breath was almost stopped and it seemed as if we glided along in the air for I could hear no sound of our footsteps. We continued on our course for a long time till we came to [a] glen surrounded by very high mountains. How we passed over those mountains I could never tell. In the middle of the glen there was a small fountain of very clear water. My conducter directed me to drink of it. This I did and imediatly I found myself in a palace the glory of which far exceeds any description which I can give. The tall stately pillars reaching from heaven to earth were formed of the finest and purest diamonds the

[32]

pavement sparkling with gold and precious stones and the mighty dome made solem and awful by its stupendous magnitude was of one single emerald. In the midst of this grand and magnificent palace was a lamp like the sun the radiance of which made all the palace to flash and glitter with an almost fearful grandeur. The ruby sent forth a stream of crimson light the topaz gold the saphire intensest purple and the dome poured a flood of deep clear splendour which overcame all the other gaudy lights by its mild triumphant glory. In this palace were thousands and tens of thousand of fairies and geni some of whom flitted lightly among the blazing lamps to the sound of unearthly music which dyed and swelled a strain of wild grandeur suited to the words they sung —

In this fairy land of light
No mortal ere has been
And the dreadful grandeur of this sight
By them hath not been seen.

T'would strike them shudering to the earth
Like the flash from a thunder cloud
It would quench their light and joyous mirth
And fit them for the shroud.

The rising of our palaces
Like visions of the deep
And the glory of their structure
No mortal voice can speak.

The music of our songs
And our mighty trumpets' swell
And the sounding of our silver harps
No mortal tongue can tell.

Of us they know but little
Save when the storm doth rise
And the mighty waves are tossing
Against the arched skys.

Then oft they see us striding
O'er the billows snow white foam
Or hear us speak in thunder
When we stand in grandeur lone

On the darkest of the mighty clouds
Which veil the pearly moon
Around us lightning flashing
Night's blackness to illume.

Chorus:
The music of our songs
And our mighty trumpets' swell
And the sounding of our silver harp[s]
No mortal tongue can tell.

When they had finished there was a dead silence for
about half an hour and then the palace began slowly
and gradualy to vanish till it disapeared intirely and I
found myself in the glen surounded by high mountains
the fountain illuminated by the cold light of the moon

[36]

springing up in the middle of the valley and standing
close by was the old man who had conducted me to this
enchanted place. He turned round and I could see that
his countenance had an expression of strange severity
which I had not before observed. "Follow me" he said.

I obeyed and we began to ascend the mountain. It would be needless to trouble you with a repitition of all my adventures. Suffice it to say that after two months time we arrived at a large temple. We entred it. The interior as well as the outside had a very gloomy and ominous aspect being intirely built of black marble. The old man suddenly seized me and dragged me to an altar at the upper end of the temple then forcing me down on my knees he made me swear that I would be his servant for ever. This promise I faithfully kept notwithstanding the dreadful scenes of magic of which every day of my life I was forced to be a witness. One day he told me that he would discharge me from the oath I had taken and comanded me to leave his service. I obeyed and after wandering about the world for many years I one evening laid myself down on a little bank by the roadside intending to pass the night there. Suddenly I felt myself raised in the air by invisible hands. In a short time I lost sight of the earth and continued on my course through the clouds till I became insensible and when I recovered from my swoon I found myself lying outside this cave. What may be my future destiny I know not".

Chapter the V

When the old man had finished his tale O Donell and Delancy thanked him for the relation adding at the same time that they had never heard anything half so wonderful. Then as it was very late they all retired to rest. Next morning O Donell awoke very early and looking round the cave he perceived the bed of leaves on which the old man had lain to be empty. Then rising he went out of the cave. The sky was covered with red fiery clouds except those in the east whose edges were tinged with the bright rays of the morning sun as they strove to hide its glory with their dark veil of vapours now all beauty and radiance by the golden line of light which streaked their gloomy surface. Beneath this storm portending sky and far off to the westward rose two tremendous rocks whose sumits were enveloped with black clouds rolling one above another with an awful magnificence well suited to the land of wilderness and mountain which they canopied. Gliding

along in the air between these two rocks was a chariot of light and in the chariot sat a figure the expression of whose countenance was that of the old man armed with the majesty and might of a spirit. O Donell stood at the mouth of the cave watching it till it vanished and then calling Delancy he related the circumstance to him. Some years after this Alexander went out one morning in search of the fruit on which they subsisted. Noon came and he had not returned; evening and still no tidings of him. O Donell began to be alarmed and set out in search of him but could nowhere find him. One whole day he spent in wandering about the rocks and mountains and in the evening he came back to his cave weary and faint with hunger and thirst. Days weeks months passed away and no Delancy apeared. O Donell might now be said to be truly miserable. He would sit on a rock for hours together and cry out "Alexander Alexander" but receive no answer except the distant echoing of his voice among the rocks. Sometimes he fancied it was another person answering him and he would listen ernestly till it dyed away then sinking into utter despair again he would sit till the dews of night began to fall when he would retire to his cave to pass the night in unquiet broken slumbers or in thinking of his beloved commander whom he could never see more. In one of these dreadful intervals he took up a small parcel and opening it he saw lying before him two locks of soft curly hair shining like burnished gold. He gazed on them for a little and thought of the words

of those who gave them to him—"Take this then that you may rember us when you dwell with only the wild beast of the desert and the great eagle of the mountain". He burst into a flood of tears he wrung his hands in sorrow and in the anguish of the moment he wished that he could once more see them and the mighty Warrior King their father if it cost him his life. Just at that instant a loud clap of thunder shook the roof of the cave a sound like the rushing of the wind was heard and a mighty genius stood before him. "I know thy wish" cried he with a loud and terrible voice "and I will grant it. In two months time thou returnest to the castle wence thou camest hither and surrenderest thyself into my power. O Donell promised that he would and instantly he found himself at the door of the old castle and in the land of his birth. He pursued his journey for three days and on the third day he arrived at the mountain which overlooked the city. It was a beautiful evening in the month of September and the full moon was shedding her tranquil light on all the face of nature. The city was lying in its splendour and magnificence surrounded by the broad stream of the Guadima. The palace was majestically towering in the midst of it and all its pillars and battlements seemed in the calm light of the moon as if they were transformed into silver by the touch of a fairy's wand. O Donell staid not long to contemplate this beautiful scene but decending the mountain he soon crossed the fertile plain which led to

the city and entering the gates he quickly arrived at the palace without speaking to anyone. He entred the inner court of the palace by a secret way with which he was acquainted and then going up a flight of steps and crossing a long gallery he arrived at the King's private apartment. The door was half open. He looked in and beheld two very handsome young men sitting together and reading. He instantly recognised them and was going to step forward when the door opened and the Great Duke entred. O Donell could contain himself no longer but rushing in he threw himself at the feet of his Grace. "O Donell is this you?" exclaimed the Duke. "It is my most noble master" answered O Donell almost choking with joy. The young princes instantly embraced him while he almost smothered them with caresses. After a while they became tranquil and then O Donell at the request of the Duke related all his adventures since he parted with them not omiting the condition on which he was now in the palace. When he had ended a loud voice was heard saying that he was free from his promise and might spend the rest of his days in his native city. Some time after this as O Donell was walking in the streets he met a gentleman who he thought he had seen before but could not recolect where or under what circumstances. After a little conversation he discovered that he was Alexander Delancy that he was now a rich merchant in the city of Paris and high in favour with the emperor Napoleon. As may be suposed they both were equally

delighted at the discovery. They ever after lived hapily in their seperate cities and so ends my little tale.

C Bronte August the 17 1829

FINIS

THE SEARCH AFTER

HAPINESS

A TALE BY

CHARLOTTE

BRONTE

PRINTED BY HERSELF

AND

SOLD BY

NOBODY &c &c

AUGUST

THE

SEVENTEENTH

▬▬▬

EIGHTEEN HUNDRED

AND O~~~~~~

Twenty nine